Ocean Maps

Coordinate Planes

Julia Wall

Publishing Credits

Editor
Sara Johnson

Editorial Director
Dona Herweck Rice

Editor-in-Chief
Sharon Coan, M.S.Ed.

Creative Director
Lee Aucoin

Publisher
Rachelle Cracchiolo, M.S.Ed.

Image Credits

The author and publisher would like to gratefully credit or acknowledge the following for permission to reproduce copyright material: cover (background, below & right) Shutterstock; p.1 Corbis; p.4 The Photolibrary; p.6 The Photolibrary; pp.7–9 Shutterstock; p.10 Alamy (above), NOAA (below); p.11 Shutterstock; p.12 Shutterstock; p.14 Alamy; p.15 NOAA; p.16 The Photolibrary; p.17 Alamy; p.18 The Photolibrary; p.19 NOAA; p.20 NOAA; p. 21 NOAA; p.22 Shutterstock; p.23 (below) Alamy, Corbis (above); p.25 The Photolibrary; p.26 The Photolibrary; p.27 Istock Photos.

Diagrams by Miranda Costa

While every care has been taken to trace and acknowledge copyright, the publishers tender their apologies for any accidental infringement where copyright has proved untraceable. They would be pleased to come to a suitable arrangement with the rightful owner in each case.

Teacher Created Materials

5301 Oceanus Drive
Huntington Beach, CA 92649-1030
http://www.tcmpub.com
ISBN 978-0-7439-0915-0

Table of Contents

Oceans
of Water

Nearly three quarters of Earth's surface is covered with water. Modern technology (tek-NOL-uh-jee) has helped us learn more about oceans than ever before. But there are large areas of ocean that are still a mystery. The world's oceans are so large and so deep that many parts have not even been mapped yet.

Ocean waves can be large and powerful.

Earth's Oceans

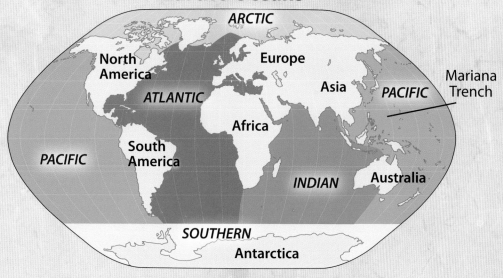

Earth has 5 oceans—the Pacific, the Atlantic, the Indian, the Arctic, and the Southern. Together, they cover an area of 138,910,300 square miles (359,776,025 km²). The deepest point is found 36,198 feet (11,033 m) under the surface of the Pacific Ocean. It is called the Mariana Trench.

Ocean Depths

Name	Deepest point (feet)	Deepest point (meters)
Arctic Ocean	15,305	4,665
Southern Ocean*	23,736	7,235
Indian Ocean	23,812	7,258
Atlantic Ocean	28,231	8,605
Pacific Ocean	36,198	11,033

* The Southern Ocean was identified and named in 2000.

Finding the Way

Sailing Earth's oceans has always been a challenge. For centuries, people have used ships to travel and carry goods from place to place. Before maps were made, sailors used **myths** and stories about past journeys to help them **navigate** (nav-uh-GAYT).

Sailors also used the stars in the night sky to find their way. To them, the sky was like a giant map. Sailors knew that in the northern **hemisphere** (HEM-uhs-feer), the Pole Star showed which way was north.

Star Light, Star Bright

The Pole Star sits above the North Pole. The Pole Star is also known as the North Star, the Steering Star, and the Ship Star. It is also called Stella Maris (STELL-uh MAR-uhs), which means "star of the sea" in Latin.

In the 12th century, many sailors started to use a tool called a compass. The compass helped the sailors to find direction. A compass shows 4 main directions: north, south, east, and west. Each direction has a location that is measured in **degrees**. North is 0° (360°), east is 90°, south is 180°, and west is 270°.

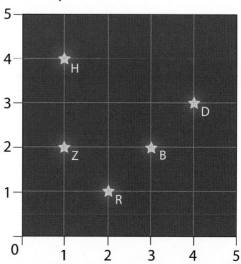

LET'S EXPLORE MATH

Using a **coordinate** (koh-ORD-uh-nuht) **plane** is kind of like using a map. **Coordinates** are a good way of finding locations. They refer to the **intersection** (in-ter-SEK-shuhn) of lines on coordinate planes. This coordinate plane shows the location of stars in the night sky. The stars are labelled with letters. Use the coordinate plane below to determine the star located at each coordinate. *Hint*: Coordinates are always read across, then up or down.

a. (1, 4)

b. (4, 3)

c. (2, 1)

d. (1, 2)

e. (3, 2)

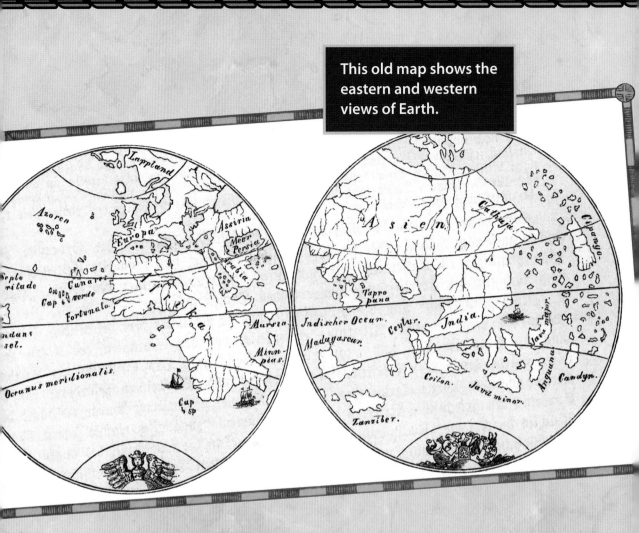

This old map shows the eastern and western views of Earth.

By the 14th century, there were many mapmakers at work. They made maps of the world based on measurements and **landmarks,** instead of stories and myths. Now sailors could find their way around the oceans much more easily.

Even after better ocean maps were made, many people still believed that Earth was flat. They thought that if you sailed far enough across the ocean, you would reach the edge of Earth and fall off!

Christopher Columbus believed Earth was round. So he sailed west from Spain to try to reach the trade routes in the Far East. Instead, he found the Americas. Almost 30 years later, Magellan's crew proved Earth was round by **circumnavigating** (sir-kuhm-NAV-uh-gayt-ing) Earth.

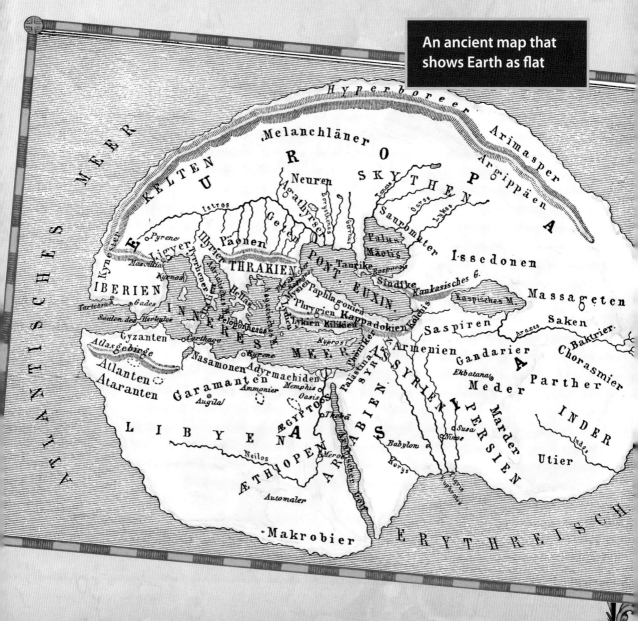

An ancient map that shows Earth as flat

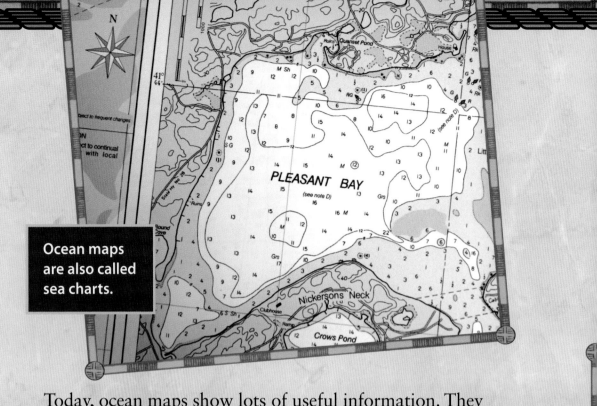

Ocean maps are also called sea charts.

Today, ocean maps show lots of useful information. They help sailors navigate and rescue people lost at sea. They help scientists protect **marine** (muh-REEN) life. They are used to forecast the weather and changes in the environment.

Marine researchers also use ocean maps to find shipwrecks on the ocean floor.

The shipwreck of the *Titanic*

Map Coordinates

Mapmakers use lines of **latitude** (LAT-uh-tood) and **longitude** (LAHN-juh-tood) to turn Earth into a huge grid. Grid coordinates are used to give the location of any place on land, or on the surface of the ocean.

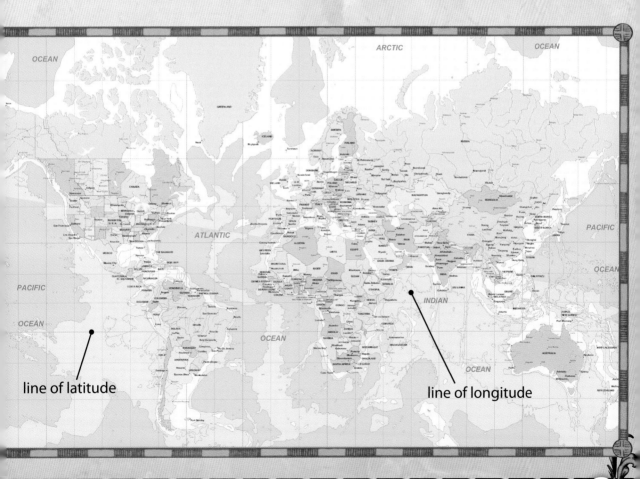

line of latitude

line of longitude

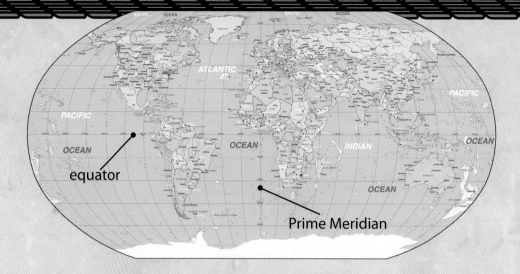

equator

Prime Meridian

Lines of latitude run **parallel** (PAIR-uh-lell) with the **equator** (ee-KWAY-ter). They tell you how far north or south of the equator a place lies. Lines of longitude run from the North Pole to the South Pole. They tell you how far east or west a place is from the **Prime Meridian** (muh-RID-ee-uhn). Latitude and longitude coordinates are measured in degrees (°). These are written as °N, °S, °E, or °W; for example, 45°W.

LET'S EXPLORE MATH

Write the coordinates of these islands:

a. Island T

b. Island X

c. Island W

d. Island L

e. Island G

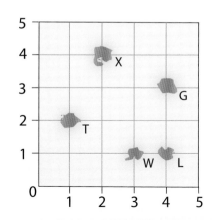

Under the Surface

To make better maps of the ocean, scientists need to find out more about the ocean floor. The ocean floor is not flat. Just like Earth's land, the ocean floor has mountains, ridges, valleys, and plains.

The first method for measuring the depth of the ocean was very simple. A line with a weight attached was lowered into the sea. The length of the line was measured when it hit the bottom.

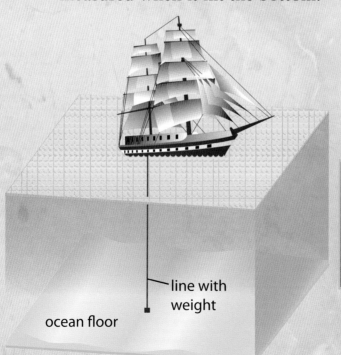

line with weight

ocean floor

This diagram shows the method used by scientists long ago when measuring the depth of the ocean.

The Secrets of Sound Waves

Later, scientists began to use **sound waves** to explore the ocean floor. They discovered that sound waves could bounce off objects under the water. They measured the time it took for the sound waves to bounce back to their measuring station.

Underwater Mountains

Did you know that the longest mountain range on Earth is found beneath the ocean? The Mid-Atlantic Ridge runs from the Arctic Ocean, down through the Atlantic Ocean. It is longer than the length of the Andes, the Rockies, and the Himalayas (him-uh-LAY-uhz) put together!

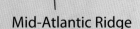

Mid-Atlantic Ridge

In the 1870s, a U.S. Navy admiral named Charles Sigsbee (SIGZ-bee) made a machine that used sound-wave technology. The Sigsbee Sounding Machine was used to create the first modern map of the Gulf of Mexico. This is one of the deepest parts of the world's oceans.

The Sigsbee Sounding Machine could only measure depth in one place at a time. Each measurement was recorded and then an **average** depth was calculated.

In the 1950s, the system of side-scan **sonar** (SOH-nar) was invented. Sonar stands for SOund NAvigation Ranging. Ships towed **sensors** deep under the water. The sensors sent sound waves out across hundreds of miles of the ocean floor. This allowed scientists to measure depth across a very big area at one time.

Today, scientists match these measurements with other data they have collected. They use computers to create 3-D maps of what Earth's sea floor looks like.

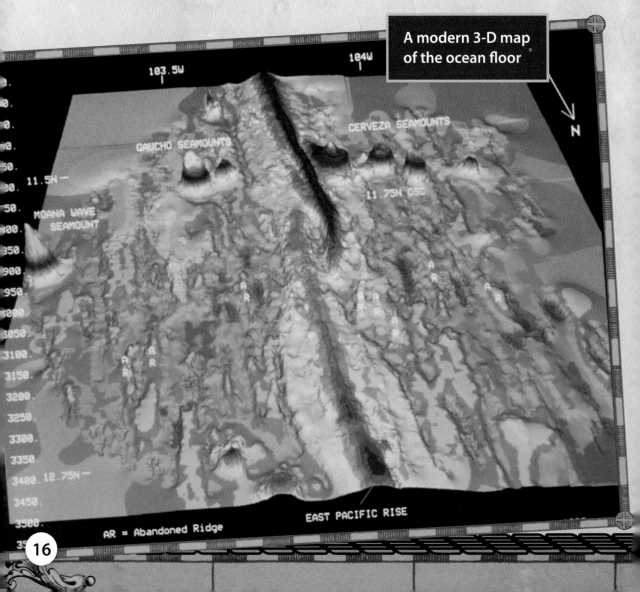

A modern 3-D map of the ocean floor

AR = Abandoned Ridge

Sonar systems are used to make ocean maps, find sea life, record ocean currents, and communicate with **submarines**.

The screen on the right of this boat uses sonar to show the depth of the water.

LET'S EXPLORE MATH

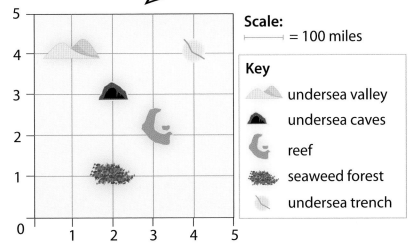

Scale:
⊢────┤ = 100 miles

Key

undersea valley

undersea caves

reef

seaweed forest

undersea trench

Use the coordinate plane, key, and scale to answer the following questions.

Give the coordinates for:

a. the undersea valley   **b.** the undersea caves

What will you find at these coordinates:

c. (2, 1)?   **d.** (3, 2)?   **e.** (4, 4)?

f. About how far is the seaweed forest from the undersea valley? *Hint*: Use the scale to figure out your answer. You cannot move diagonally.

17

New Ways of Seeing the Sea

In the 1960s, three new tools were developed to find out more about the ocean. The first was the near-bottom sonar system called Deep Tow. With this system, a sensor is lowered from a boat to sit just above the ocean floor. The sensor gathers data about the angles at which the ocean floor slopes.

A Deep Tow sensor is lowered into the ocean.

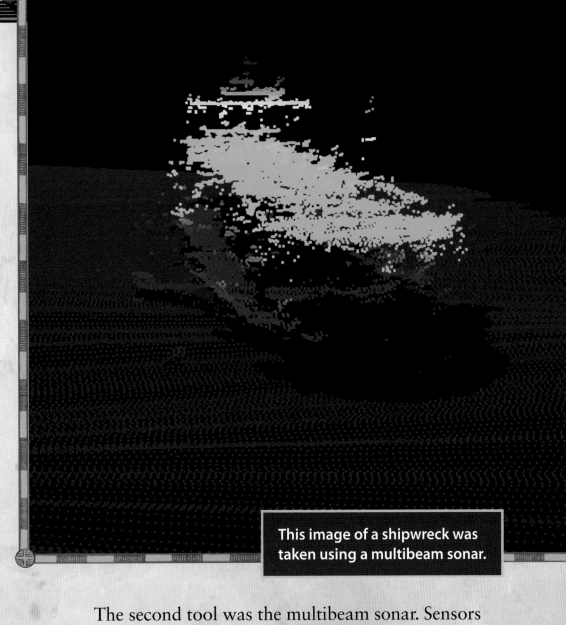

This image of a shipwreck was taken using a multibeam sonar.

The second tool was the multibeam sonar. Sensors attached to the bottom of a ship send out beams in a fan shape. The beams collect information about the depth of the ocean and what the ocean floor is made of. This data is combined with latitude and longitude coordinates to make very accurate maps of the ocean floor.

The third tool was the **submersible** (sub-MER-suh-buhl). Scientists use these small underwater vehicles to explore the ocean floor up close. A submersible uses a single sonar beam that moves at many angles to the sea floor. A lot of information is gathered from a small area.

A submersible

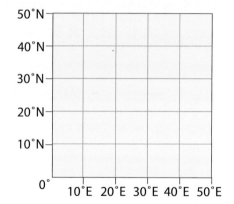

Create your own map. Draw this coordinate plane. Mark on your coordinate plane to show the following:

a a shipwreck located at (10°E, 40°N).

b. a group of sharp rocks located at (40°E, 30°N).

c. a reef located at (20°E, 10°N).

d. an island located at (30°E, 40°N)

Create a key to explain the content added to your coordinate plane.

The first submersibles carried scientists and researchers deep into the ocean. Today, scientists use ROVs. ROV stands for Remotely Operated Vehicle. People do not travel in them. ROVs have cameras and sensors that collect information on latitude, longitude, and depth. They can travel to depths of 20,000 feet (6,096 m)!

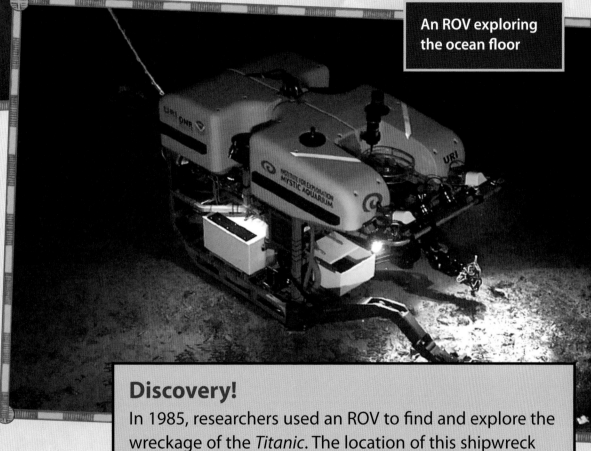

An ROV exploring the ocean floor

Discovery!

In 1985, researchers used an ROV to find and explore the wreckage of the *Titanic*. The location of this shipwreck had been a mystery for more than 70 years.

The film director James Cameron used a submersible to shoot parts of his movie, *Titanic*. It traveled 12,378 feet (3,773 m) below the Atlantic Ocean.

Eyes in the Sky

GPS technology uses information from **satellites** (SAT-uh-lites) to find any place on Earth quickly and accurately. GPS stands for Global Positioning System. There are 24 satellites used for GPS. Computers need to get signals from at least 3 of these satellites to find latitude and longitude coordinates.

GPS technology can be used on ships, in planes, and even in cars! It works in any weather, anywhere in the world, 24 hours a day.

A GPS satellite **orbits** the Earth.

A researcher marks an underwater site of a shipwreck using metal stakes and colored string.

When researchers find the site of a shipwreck, they use GPS technology onboard their ships to record its latitude and longitude coordinates. This means they can return to the site without relying on memory or landmarks that can change over time. Sailors lost at sea can use **portable** (POR-tuh-buhl) GPS tools to send their locations to rescue teams.

A rescue at sea

GPS technology can find a location on the ocean's surface, but it cannot find a location under the water. To do this, scientists must use GIS technology. GIS stands for Geographic Information Systems.

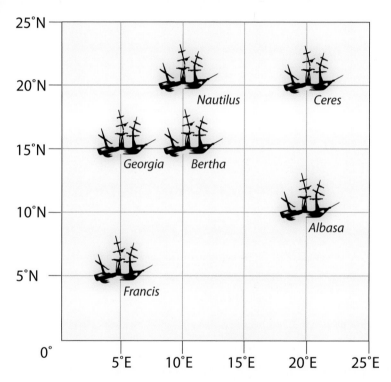

This map shows the shipwrecks along Shipwreck Coast. Write the locations of each wreck using the latitude and longitude references.

GIS uses underwater data from sonar systems and surface data from GPS. It also uses data about the ocean floor. All this information is put together to make 3-D maps of the sea floor. These maps help scientists to understand and predict how the ocean behaves. Scientists can also use this information to learn about life in the ocean. They can learn about where marine animals live and how many there are in an area.

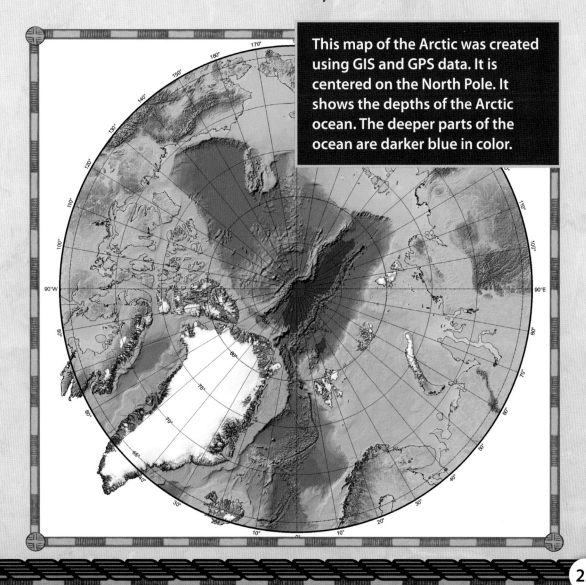

This map of the Arctic was created using GIS and GPS data. It is centered on the North Pole. It shows the depths of the Arctic ocean. The deeper parts of the ocean are darker blue in color.

The Changing Tide of Technology

Many years ago, ocean exploration and sailing was very difficult. Sailing the Earth's oceans can still be challenging. But modern ocean technology helps sailors to navigate more easily. Marine researchers can also find a location in the ocean and measure its depth quickly and accurately.

This is a 3-D image of the sea floor near Los Angeles in the United States. Scientists can use this kind of sea map to study areas where underwater earthquakes may occur.

The technology used today to map the ocean floor is far more advanced than the first weighted lines sent to the bottom of the ocean. Today, researchers know far more than just the depths of the oceans. They can create maps that show us what the ocean floor looks like. And we can learn about the marine life that lives beneath the ocean's surface.

Shipwreck Coast

You have been given a coordinate plane map. It shows the location of shipwrecks in a small but dangerous area of the ocean. It also shows the location of sunken treasure.

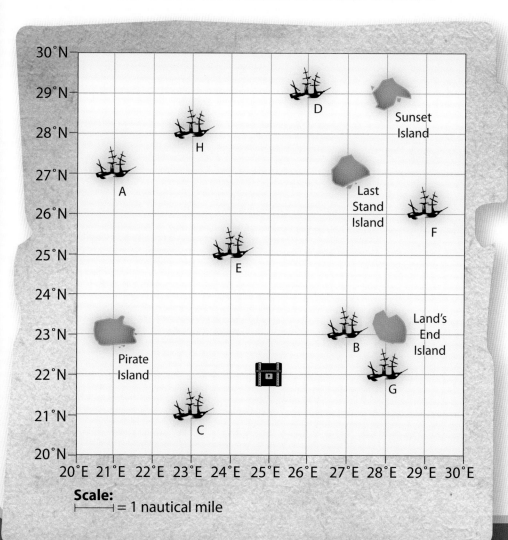

Scale:
⊢————⊣ = 1 nautical mile

Solve It!

Use the coordinate plane map to answer these questions.

a. Write the coordinates for each shipwreck.

b. Which island is at the coordinates (27°E, 27°N)?

c. Which island would you be on if you were at (28°E, 23°N)?

Now use the scale and the sea chart to answer these questions. *Hint*: You can move across or up and down, not diagonally.

d. About how many nautical miles from Last Stand Island was Shipwreck F before it sank?

e. About how many nautical miles is Sunset Island from Shipwreck D?

Records tell us that the ships were looking for sunken treasure.

f. Which ships were closest to the treasure when they sank? Give the distances.

g. Which ship was farthest from the treasure when it sank? How far away was it?

Glossary

average—the total of the numbers in a set divided by the amount of numbers in a set

circumnavigating—steering a ship on a course around Earth

coordinate plane—a plane with 2 axes, *x* and *y*, used to graph coordinates

coordinates—numbered points on a coordinate plane

degrees—units of measurement that show direction and location

equator—an imaginary line around the center of Earth

hemisphere—the northern or southern half of Earth

intersection—the point where 2 lines cross

landmarks—reference points such as islands or coastlines

latitude—the distance of a location north or south

longitude—the distance of a location east or west

marine—having to do with the sea

myths—legends from the past

navigate—to steer on a set course

orbits—circles around Earth in space

parallel—in the same direction; will never intersect

portable—able to be carried or moved about

Prime Meridian—the meridian of 0° longitude from which other longitudes are calculated

satellites—objects sent into space, by scientists, that orbit other bodies and send signals back to Earth

sensors—objects that send out and collect signals

sonar—an object that sends out sound waves and collects signals

sound waves—the invisible patterns made by sounds as they travel through water or air

submarines—vessels that can travel above or below the water

submersible—a vehicle that travels underwater

Index

Let's Explore Math

Page 7:

a. Star H

b. Star D

c. Star R

d. Star Z

e. Star B

Page 12:

a. (1, 2)

b. (2, 4)

c. (3, 1)

d. (4, 1)

e. (4, 3)

Page 17:

a. (1, 4)

b. (2, 3)

c. seaweed forest

d. reef

e. undersea trench

f. about 400 miles

Page 20:

Symbols will vary but layout should follow the format below.

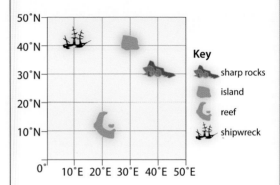

Page 24:

Georgia: (5°E, 15°N)

Francis: (5°E, 5°N)

Bertha: (10°E, 15°N)

Nautilus: (10°E, 20 °N)

Ceres: (20°E, 20°N)

Albasa: (20°E, 10°N)

Problem-Solving Activity

a. Wreck A: (21°E, 27°N); Wreck B: (27°E, 23°N); Wreck C: (23°E, 21°N); Wreck D: (26°E, 29°N); Wreck E: (24°E, 25°N); Wreck F: (29°E, 26°N); Wreck G: (28°E, 22°N); Wreck H: (23˚E, 28˚N)

b. Last Stand Island

c. Land's End Island

d. about 3 nautical miles

e. about 2 nautical miles

f. Ships G, C, and B were closest to the treasure. They were all about 3 nautical miles from the treasure.

g. Ship A was the farthest from the treasure. It was about 9 nautical miles away.